First Experiences

GOING TO
THE HOSPITAL

Anne Civardi
Illustrated by Stephen Cartwright
Medical Consultant: Edward Mee, FRCS
Reading Consultant: Betty Root

There is a little yellow duck hiding on every two pages. Can you find it?

The Bells

This is the Bell family. Ben is six and Bess is three.
Ben is not feeling very well. He has earache.

Doctor Small

DR. SMALL

The next day Mom takes Ben to see Dr. Small. He says that Ben needs to have an operation on his sore ear.

In the Hospital

Ben goes to the hospital for his operation.
There are lots of other children in the ward.

Mom helps Ben put on his pyjamas and unpack his suitcase. Nurse Potter helps him too.

Nurse Potter

Nurse Potter tucks Ben in bed. She takes his temperature and pulse to make sure they are normal.

Then she checks his blood pressure with a special machine. She writes down the results on Ben's chart.

Dr. Hart, the Surgeon

DR. HART

Dr. Hart, the surgeon, will operate on Ben's sore ear.
She comes in to see him and tells him all about it.

Before the Operation

Nurse Potter gives Ben an injection to make him feel nice and sleepy before he has his operation.

Bob, the Orderly

BOB

Bob, the orderly, helps Ben on to a gurney. Then he wheels him down to the operating room.

The Anaesthetist

Before the operation Ben breathes in some gas. He will sleep soundly while Dr. Hart operates on his ear.

Back in the Ward

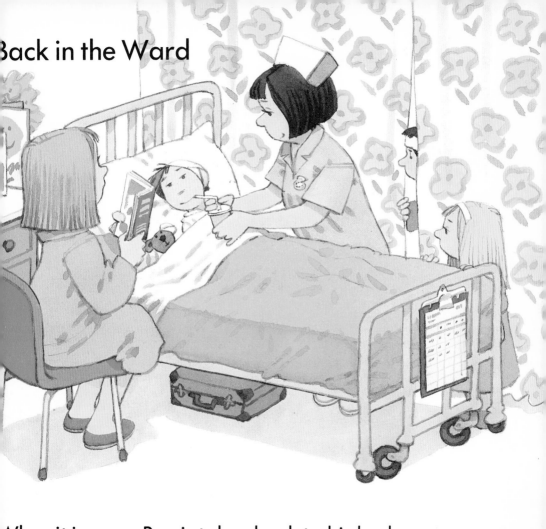

When it is over, Ben is taken back to his bed.
He is still sleepy but his ear is much better.

Feeling Better

The next morning Ben feels even better. He can get out of bed now and play with his new friends.

en eats lots of lunch. He is very hungry because he did
ot eat anything on the day of his operation.

Visiting Time

After lunch Mom, Dad and Granny come to see Ben.
Ben shows Dad his ear. He is very proud of it.

Granny has brought Ben a new car for being so brave.
The other children have visitors too.

Going Home

The next day Ben is ready to go home. His earache has gone. He says goodbye to Nurse Potter and Dr. Hart.

First published in 1986
Usborne Publishing Ltd
20 Garrick St, London
WC2 9BJ, England
© Usborne Publishing Ltd 1986

The name of Usborne and the
device are Trade Marks of
Usborne Publishing Ltd.
American Edition 1986
Printed in Portugal